THE HARDEST WORD

A
Yom Kippur
Story

by Jacqueline Jules
illustrated by
Katherine Janus Kahn

KAR-BEN
PUBLISHING

In loving memory of my parents, Jeanne and Otto Selig.
JJ

To my publishers.
KJK

Author's Note

This story is loosely based on a Hasidic legend "The Tear of Repentance."

The **Ziz** comes from Jewish folklore and was considered to be the king of all the birds.

Yom Kippur — Day of Atonement. This holy day, which comes ten days after Rosh Hashanah, the Jewish New Year, is the holiest day of the Jewish year. Adults and children over the age of Bar/Bat Mitzvah fast and spend the day in synagogue offering prayers of repentance. In addition to asking forgiveness, however, one who has harmed another person is expected to offer restitution and make amends.

Sukkot — Festival of Booths. Five days after Yom Kippur, this joyous festival of the harvest is celebrated. To recall the 40 years the Israelites wandered in the desert after leaving Egypt, families build sukkot — booths — to recall the temporary shelters in the desert. The booths are decorated with fruits and vegetables. Families eat holiday meals in the sukkah.

Mt. Sinai is the mountain Moses ascended to receive the Ten Commandments. The Ziz chooses to talk over his mistakes at the place where God revealed the rules we live by.

Text copyright © 2001 by Jacqueline Jules
Illustrations copyright © 2001 by Katherine Janus Kahn

Kar-Ben Publishing
A division of Lerner Publishing Group, Inc.
241 First Avenue North
Minneapolis, MN 55401 U.S.A.
1-800-4KARBEN

Website address: www.karben.com

Library of Congress Cataloging-in-Publication Data

Jules, Jacqueline, 1956–
    The hardest word: a Yom Kippur story / Jacqueline Jules; illustrated by Katherine Janus Kahn.
        p.   cm.
    Summary: The Ziz, a huge bird that is clumsy but good-hearted, accidentally destroys a vegetable garden and when he asks God for advice he learns the importance of apologizing.
        ISBN-13: 978–1–58013–030–1 (lib. bdg. : alk. paper)
        ISBN-10: 1–58013–030–5 (lib. bdg. : alk. paper)
        ISBN-13: 978–1–58013–028–8 (pbk. : alk. paper)
        ISBN-10: 1–58013–028–3 (pbk. : alk. paper)
        [1. Apologizing—Fiction. 2. Animals, Mythical—Fiction. 3. Jews—Fiction.] I. Kahn, Katherine, ill. II. Title.
    PZ7.J92947Har 2001
    [E]—dc21   2001029626

Manufactured in the United States of America
2 – CG – 6/1/2010

A LONG, LONG TIME AGO

the world had many large and fabulous creatures.

One of those creatures
was a gigantic yellow
bird with dark red
wings and a purple
forehead.

He was called the Ziz.

The Ziz was so huge that when he spread out his wings,
he blocked the sun, as if he were a dark rain cloud.
Every time he flew over a town, all the mothers
would call to their children, "Come
inside quickly before it rains."
This made the big Ziz sad.
He loved children, and
didn't want to spoil
their playtime.

So the Ziz started flying around at night, when no one
would notice that he made the sky dark with his gigantic wings.
That worked fine for a while. Then one night, the big Ziz flew
too high and he bumped into a star.

Sizzle!
Snap!
Bang!

The star fell out of the sky
and down to earth.
It burned a big hole in the ground.

The next morning, when the Ziz saw the big hole, he was worried. "What can I do to cover this hole?" he asked himself. He thought about it for awhile and came up with an idea. He stretched out his huge wings and went back up into the sky. This time, he knocked down a cloud. Plop! The cloud was full of rain and it filled the big hole with water. Now the big hole was a lovely pond, perfect for swimming.

All the children came running to the pond, screaming with delight. It was a hot, sunny day and they had a wonderful time splashing and playing in the water.

"That mistake is all fixed." The Ziz smiled.

One day, however, the Ziz made a mistake he could not fix. It was the week before Yom Kippur. He was flying along, not watching where he was going, and he flew smack into the tallest pine tree in the world. Boom! The tree fell over and knocked over another tree. That tree knocked down another tree and that tree fell on the vegetable garden behind the synagogue.

Smash! Squash! Oops!

"Oh no!" The Ziz covered his eyes with his big wings. "Not the vegetable garden! It belongs to the children!"

The Ziz uncovered his eyes to look at the damage. The tomatoes, the corn, the pumpkins, the beans, the gourds, the squash—all the vegetables the children had worked so hard to plant were smashed to bits.

"I can't knock down a cloud and fix this!" the Ziz cried.

The Ziz flew home and sat in his own garden to think. He had watched the children plant their vegetable garden. Every year they harvested the fruits to decorate their sukkah.

"What would the children do this year?"

The Ziz spread out his big wings and flew off to have a chat with God. The Ziz had a special place where he liked to talk to God. It was Mt. Sinai. The Ziz was so huge that when he stood on Mt. Sinai, his purple-feathered head reached right up into heaven.

"What have you done this time?" God asked as soon as he saw the Ziz. This was not the first time the Ziz had come to Mt. Sinai after making a mistake.

"I knocked over a big tree. It knocked over another tree. That tree smashed a vegetable garden."

"The children's garden?" God questioned.

"Yes," the Ziz admitted, hanging his head.

"That's a problem," God said.

"I can't knock down a cloud and make this better."

"No, you can't," God agreed.

"What should I do?"

"I want you to do something for me," God said.

"Anything," the Ziz promised.

"I want you to search the earth and bring back the hardest word."

"The hardest word?" the Ziz questioned.

"Yes," God answered. "Now go!"

The Ziz stretched his big wings and went off to search.

He flew over mountains....................He flew over trees..............

Flap! Flap! I'm the biggest bird.
Flap! Flap! Searching for the hardest word.

After searching the whole day, the Ziz stopped to rest at the edge
of a forest. In a little house nearby, he heard a mother and child arguing.

.................He flew over valleys.....................He flew over seas.

"I don't want to go to bed," the little boy said.

"You need your rest," the mother said.

"I'm not tired!" the little boy cried.

"Goodnight!" the mother said firmly, closing the door.

"That's it!" Ziz flapped his wings. "The hardest word! I found it!"

Ziz flew as fast as he could to Mt. Sinai. With great excitement he put his bird feet down on the top and poked his purple-feathered head up into heaven.

"I found it! I found the hardest word!"

"What is it?" God asked.

"It's GOODNIGHT. Every child hates that word."

Ziz did a dance right on top of Mt. Sinai. He loved being right.

"Goodnight is a hard word for children," God agreed.

"I knew it! I knew it!" Ziz danced.

"But there is another word, even harder," God said.

"There is?" Ziz slumped over, disappointed.

"There is!" God declared. "Go and find it!"

So the Ziz spread out his mighty wings and went off to search.

He flew over mountains....................He flew over trees...............

Flap! Flap! I'm the biggest bird.
Flap! Flap! Searching for the hardest word.

After searching all day, Ziz stopped at a big feast on the grounds of a castle. He listened. With so many people talking, he felt sure someone would say the hardest word.

....................*He flew over valleys*.......................*He flew over seas.*

"I'm hungry," a little girl said to her mother. "May I have some pisghetti, please?"

The mother smiled. "Oh! You want SPA-ghetti."

"That's it!" Ziz realized. "I've got it now!"

SPA

He spread out his great big wings and flew back to Mt. Sinai. He planted his bird feet on the mountaintop and poked his purple-feathered head into heaven.

"I know the hardest word," he sang.
"What is it?" God asked.

"It's SPAGHETTI!"

Ziz hopped up and down on one foot. Standing still was hard, especially when he was excited.

"Spaghetti is a hard word to say," God agreed.

"Didn't I tell you?" Ziz hopped some more.

"But there is another word, even harder," God said.

"There is?" Ziz slumped over, disappointed.

"There is!" God declared. "Go out and find it."

The Ziz stretched his big wings and went back out to search.

He flew over mountains, he flew over trees,
He flew over valleys, he flew over seas.
Flap! Flap! I'm the biggest bird.
Flap! Flap! Searching for the hardest word.

The Ziz searched for three more days. He brought back lots of words to Mt. Sinai—words like ROCK, RHINOCEROS, RIDICULOUS, and RUMPLESTILTSKIN. Each time, God sent the Ziz back out to find another word.

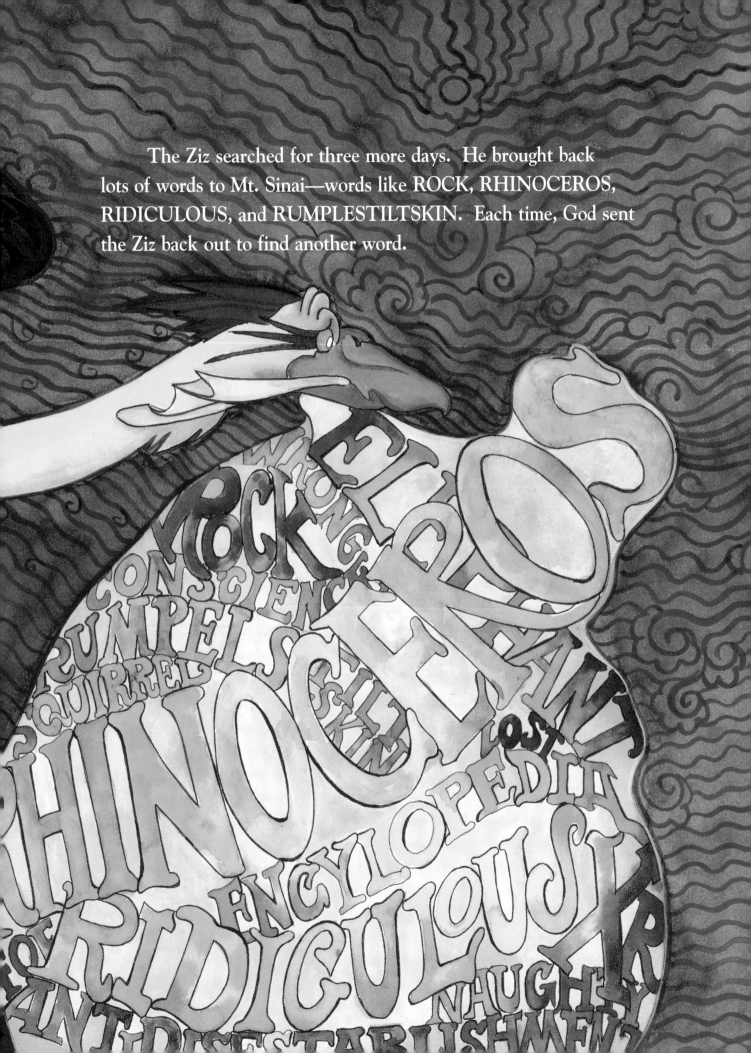

By the evening of Yom Kippur, the Ziz had brought over 100 words to Mt. Sinai. God had not accepted any of them. The Ziz was discouraged. He had tried and tried. He flew back to Mt. Sinai to have one more discussion with God.

"What word did you bring this time?" God asked.

"No word," the Ziz said quietly.

"No word?" God asked.

"No," the Ziz said sadly. "I've come to say I'm sorry. I can't find the hardest word."

"You can't?" God asked.

"No," the Ziz shook his head. "I'm sorry."

"You're sorry?" God asked.

"Yes." Ziz nodded his big purple head. "I'm sorry."

"Good job!" God said. "You found the hardest word!"

"I did?" Now the Ziz was confused.

"Yes," God said. "The hardest word is SORRY. While all the words you brought me were hard, 'sorry' is the hardest."

"I always say 'I'm sorry' on Yom Kippur," the Ziz said.

"Well, you should say it other times, too." God answered.

"Like when I smashed the garden?" Ziz asked.

"That's right," God said.

The Ziz thanked God and pulled his purple-feathered head out of heaven. Then he spread out his great big wings and flew back to the children's garden. On the way, he stopped at his own garden and gathered a big basket of fruits and vegetables for the children.

It was time to say the hardest word.